CW00859582

A PICNIC IN THE SUN

BERTIE AND FRIENDS HIT THE ROAD

Story and Songs **Christiane Duchesne** and **Jérôme Minière** Illustrations **Marianne Ferrer**
Singers **Clerel** and **Geneviève Toupin** Narration **Mischa Cheeseman**

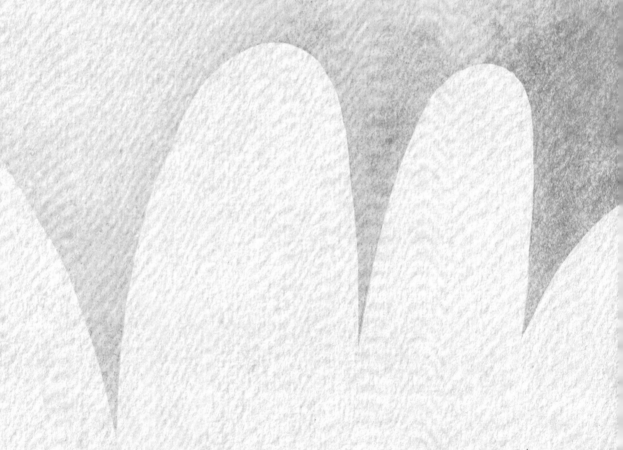

Once upon a time there were four friends who always had oodles and oodles of fun together. They were never apart. They always played together, they always ate together, they always sang together and all four of them lived together in a great big house.

There was **Bertie**, the most inquisitive one.

Then **Carl Martin Alexander**, the wisest one. We called him Marty. It was easier to call him **Marty**.

2 BERTIE AND FRIENDS

We're Bertie's friends, yes we are!
The greatest friends in the world!
No bigger than a nut
Taratata
Taratata

We're Bertie's friends, yes we are!
The greatest friends in the world!
And we will never be apart
Taratata
Taratata

Then **Maggie**,
the tallest of the four.

And **Minnie** was
the smallest one.

For days, weeks and months, they were bored to tears, because it had been raining in their land for one hundred days. One hundred days! That's a lot of rain, that's a long time, a very long time!

3 YELLOW BOOTS

One foot in the water
The other on the path
One foot in the water
The other on a pebble
One foot in the water
The other in the grass

Rain's a-falling
Lightning's a-flashing
Thunder's a-rumbling
I'm on the run

Both of my feet
In my yellow boots

4 PUDDLES O' WATER

Puddles o' water
With fish that go swimming

- Oh no, oh no!

Puddles o' water
With planes that go flying

- No, no! No, no!

Puddles o' water
With houses that go floating

- No, no, no! No, no, no!

Puddles o' water
Puddles o' water
Puddles o' water
They only have water!

- Good thing you've put your yellow boots on!

One day, Minnie had the most fabulous
idea in her whole life. On that morning,
she declared: "We'll go and have a picnic!
Let's hit the road!"

But where can you go to have a picnic
when it's been raining for one hundred days,
the rivers are overflowing, and everything
is wet, soaked, and soggy?

5 A HORSE

A horse of your dreams
An albino horse
A pine rocking horse

A flying winged horse
A sea horse so free
A wild frisky horse
A horse of your dreams
To gallop to the end of the earth
With you ...

Run away
Won't you run away?
Run away

On a mountain!

On a mountain sheltered from the rain!

Luckily enough, the Blue Mountain was soaring skyward, just over there. Maggie suggested riding there on horseback and straight away, Bertie whistled for the horses, who galloped up to meet them.

Marty chose the albino horse, Minnie chose the black one, Maggie, the dappled one, and Bertie, the big striped horse.

They set out for the Blue Mountain, the one soaring skyward, over there. They had been trotting along the wet, soaked and soggy road for at least an hour, along the banks of a wide river, when they noticed a shipwreck…

"It's an old pirate ship!" declared Bertie.
"I'm sure of it!" And even though the pirates
had vanished, they really had left a ship behind,
a very, very long time ago, the proof they
had once existed…

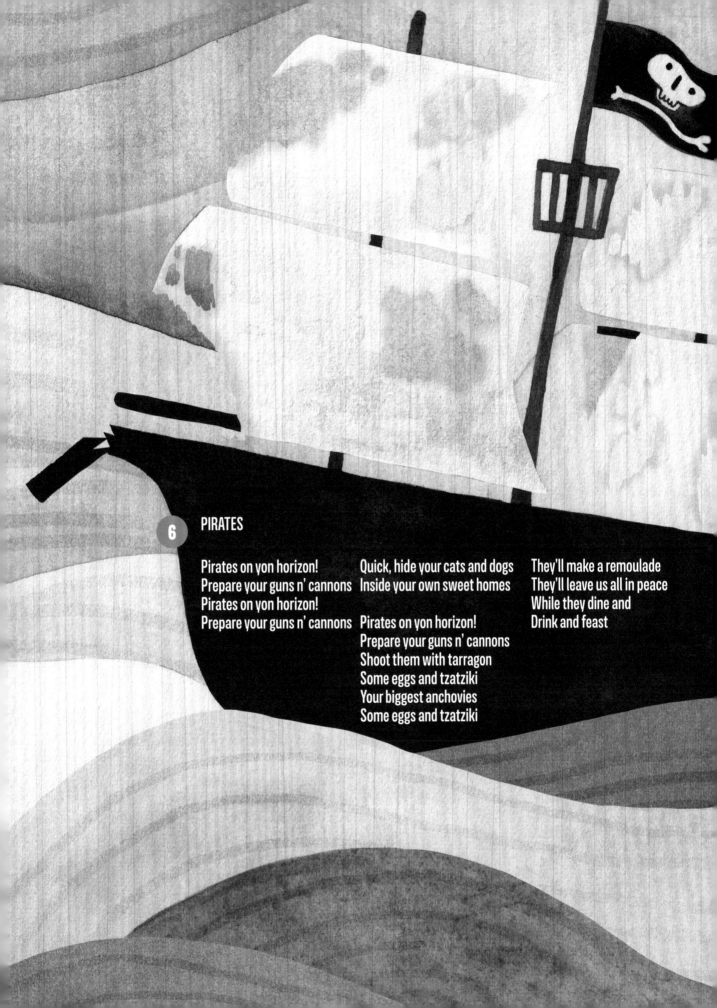

6 PIRATES

Pirates on yon horizon!
Prepare your guns n' cannons
Pirates on yon horizon!
Prepare your guns n' cannons

Quick, hide your cats and dogs
Inside your own sweet homes

Pirates on yon horizon!
Prepare your guns n' cannons
Shoot them with tarragon
Some eggs and tzatziki
Your biggest anchovies
Some eggs and tzatziki

They'll make a remoulade
They'll leave us all in peace
While they dine and
Drink and feast

Oh, yes! They would repair this old wreck
of a pirate ship, cross the river and continue
on their way to the Blue Mountain…
still soaring skyward, over there.

They decided to fit the wreck with a rudder,
wheels, and wings as well.

They added a tall mast, sails and a roof,
in case it rained forever and even for eternity.

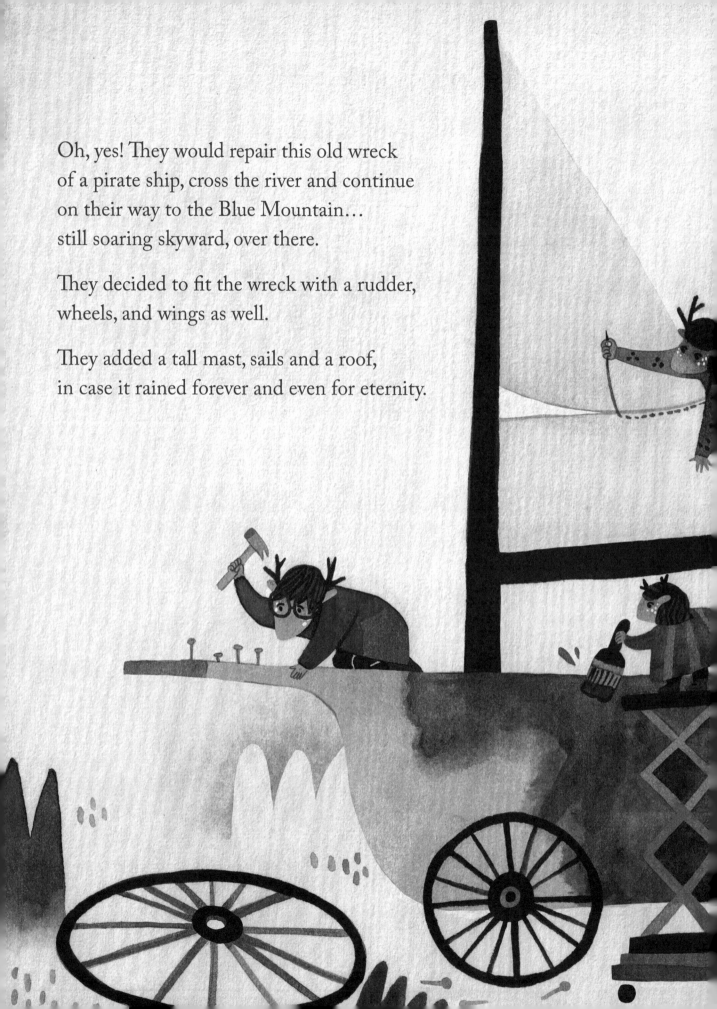

7 MICHAEL ROW THE BOAT ASHORE

Michael row the boat ashore, Hallelujah
My brothers and sisters are all aboard, Hallelujah
The river is deep and the river is wide, Hallelujah
Milk and honey on the other side, Hallelujah

Equipped with hammers, saws and all kinds of nails, they worked for two days and three nights. Marty, Minnie, Maggie and Bertie turned the shipwreck into a kind of wagon-boat so large, and so enormous, that they could board the horses, and invite friends, animals and Martians… and maybe even ghosts.

Everyone joined in a festive parade to board the boat,
the strange boat that would safely ferry them across
the river.

The wagon-boat bravely sailed on the wild water.
What a long and difficult crossing it was! Oh my!
Waves splashed through the windows and the hatches.

But when at last they arrived on the other side
of the river, the rain had completely stopped!

Bertie furled the sails and put away the rudder
while Minnie got out the wheels.

Everything was going great until suddenly…

"Stop! Stop everything!"

8 THE LADYBIRD'S SONG

Ladybird Ladybird
Ladybird Ladybird
Unfurl your wings Unfurl your wings
And fly away I'm going with you

A giant ladybird had just climbed out of a bush
and loomed in front of them.

Enchanted by the wagon-boat, the ladybird asked
them to take her with them. Bertie agreed right away.
Since the wagon-boat was really very big, and since
they were taking a ladybird on board, couldn't they
also bring other animals on board? And that is how,
on the road to the Blue Mountain (which fortunately
still soared skyward, over there), they brought
along with them a sheep, a goat, a turkey, a pig,
a cat, some ducks, a dog and a fox, a hen, a rooster,
two geese, a wolf, a weasel, a magpie
and a donkey.

9 ALL IN SINGLE FILE

The sheep walks at the front
The goat follows behind
And now the turkey struts
And then the mother pig
Then softly pads the cat
Then all the waddling ducks
The trotting dog and fox

The hen and the two geese
The magpie, wolf and mule
And as they go, they dance

All in single file
All in single file
All in single file

THE WOLF, THE FOX AND THE WEASEL

10

I saw the wolf, the fox and the weasel
I saw the wolf and the fox dancing
I saw the wolf, the fox and the weasel
I saw the wolf and the fox dancing
I saw them a-tapping their feet
I saw the wolf and the fox dancing

I saw them a-tapping their feet
I saw the wolf, the fox and the weasel

They rolled along amazing roads, bound for
the Blue Mountain that… still soared skyward,
over there. Every time they met an animal, they
would take it on board. They had so much fun,
especially when they welcomed a mute lion,
and later, a pair of acrobatic pink flamingos.

The road was lined with palm trees as pink as the
flamingos. The cut hay and apple tree flowers smelled
lovely. Everyone was laughing, singing and chattering
until night began to fall, while the moon gently rose,
smiling. The moon doesn't smile every night, but that
night, oh yes, it grinned from ear to ear.

BRAHM'S LULLABY

Lullaby and good night
With pink roses bedight
With lilies over spread
Is my baby's sweet head
Lay thee down now and rest
May thy slumber be blessed
Lay thee down now and rest
May thy slumber be blessed

Lullaby and good night
You're your mother's delight
Shining angels beside
My darling abide
Soft and warm is your bed
Close your eyes, rest your head
Soft and warm is your bed
Close your eyes, rest your head

Sleepyhead, close your eyes
Mother's right here beside you
I'll protect you from harm
You will wake in my arms
Guardian angels are near
So sleep on with no fear
Guardian angels are near
So sleep on with no fear

Bertie closed the doors and windows of the wagon-boat.
Marty, Minnie and Maggie were so excited that they put on
their pyjamas inside out.

"Everyone off to bed! Goodnight kisses!"

12 MY PYJAMAS

My pyjamas	That I'll have
When I put them on	That I'll have
Cosy n' warm	Three stories
Cosy n' warm	Two kisses and a
I know that I'll have	Lullaby...

Maggie was too excited by this amazing, fantastic voyage
they were on, and she didn't want to go to sleep, or close her eyes,
at all. So Minnie sang her a very pretty song.

13 ALBERT

A tiny little monster	- Oh, how lucky!
Lives under my bed	- I'm afraid of monsters.
His name is Albert	- But my monster is really nice.
His eyes are green	- Will you lend me your Albert?
And they light up at night	- Nope, he's my monster, he's mine!
So I'm not afraid	- Oh darn.
Of the dark any more	

And now, the horses, the hens, the wolf and all the others also wanted to have a monster like Albert living under their beds. But no matter how much they protested, their eyelids closed, sleep crept over them all, a great silence descended, and then you could hear…

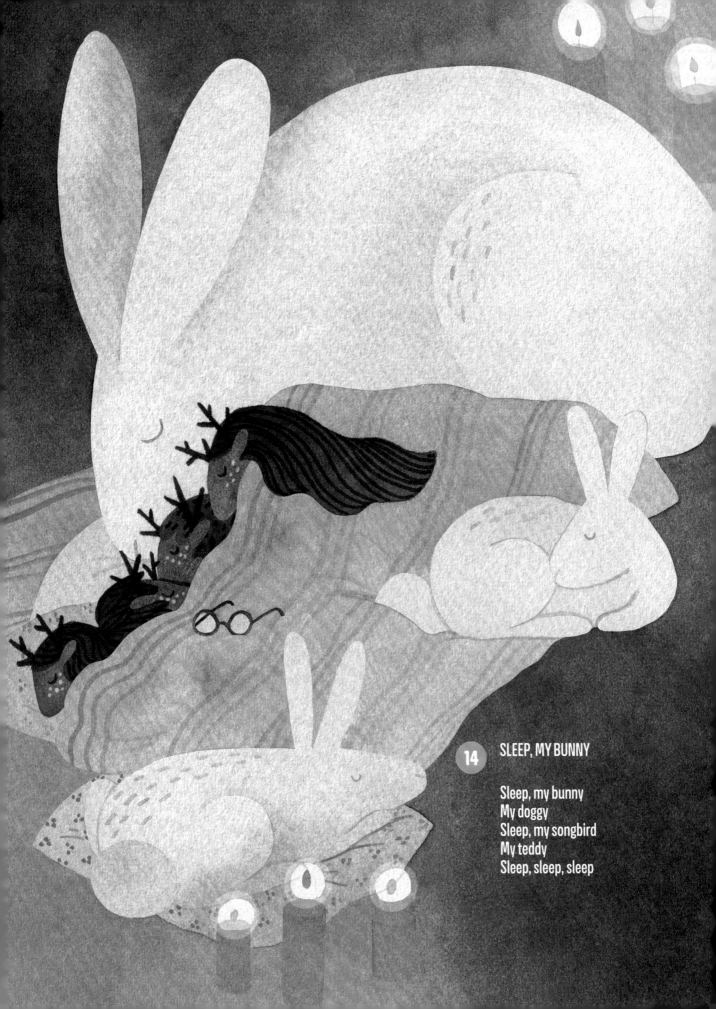

14 SLEEP, MY BUNNY

Sleep, my bunny
My doggy
Sleep, my songbird
My teddy
Sleep, sleep, sleep

15 ALL THROUGH THE NIGHT

While the moon her watch is keeping
All through the night
While the weary world is sleeping
All through the night

Breathes a pure and holy feeling
All through the night
O'er thy spirit gently stealing
Visions of delight revealing

At the end of night, that pretty time of day known
as dawn, just before the sun woke up, the early risers,
the dog, the fox and the wolf, were the only ones
who heard the enchanting chorus of the little frogs.

16 FROG SYMPHONY

Night-time has returned
The moon is up above
Over the river's waters
You will see a thousand stars
And in the trees, you'll hear
The wind singing far off
Far off, deep in the woods

You'll hear the nightbirds
Sing your song
And then a little cry
A hundred little cries
The laughter of an owl
No, no, no, no, no, no
It's a frog symphony...
They're welcoming the night

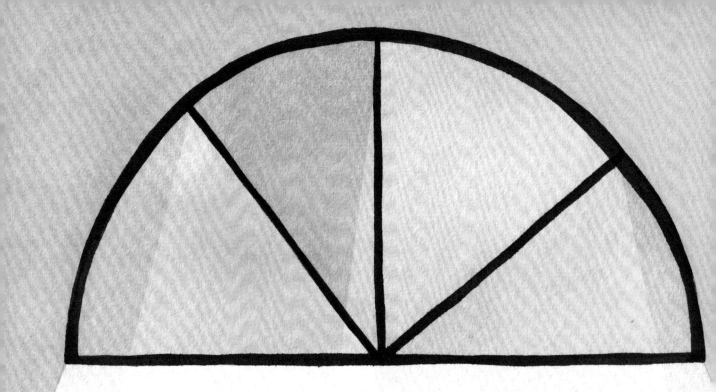

Then at last, very gently, the sun decided to rise, and the night sky became a magnificent day sky, all bathed in orange and pink. Marty, Minnie, Maggie and Bertie all opened their eyes at the same time. They were waiting for the rooster to launch into his morning song, but the rooster woke up with a very sore throat! What a shame! The pink flamingos suggested he eat raw shrimp, but there were none to be had, not in the wagon-boat kitchen or set aside for the picnic.

17 COCK-A-DOODLE-DOO

The rooster's got a sore throat
The rooster just can't crow
But who will wake us up?
The rooster's got a sore throat
The rooster just can't crow
We'll take care of our bro!

Cock, cock, cock-a-doodle-do

18 A DAY

A day is very long
Wakes up with the sun
Goes to bed late with the moon
In between that, it stretches...
While it slowly stretches out...

We jump up
We laugh
We eat
We dance
We pee

We sing as well
We run in the garden
Then we play some games
'Til night-time!

It looked like the Blue Mountain had tiptoed closer during the night, because now, it seemed to be right beside them. Maybe mountains travel quietly at night, while everyone is sleeping? Or maybe the wagon-boat managed to move along all by itself? We'll never know. Anyway, they were nearly at the foot of the mountain, and a good thing, too!

What an amazing day for the picnic they were going to have, and soon!

"Let's hit the road!" exclaimed Bertie.

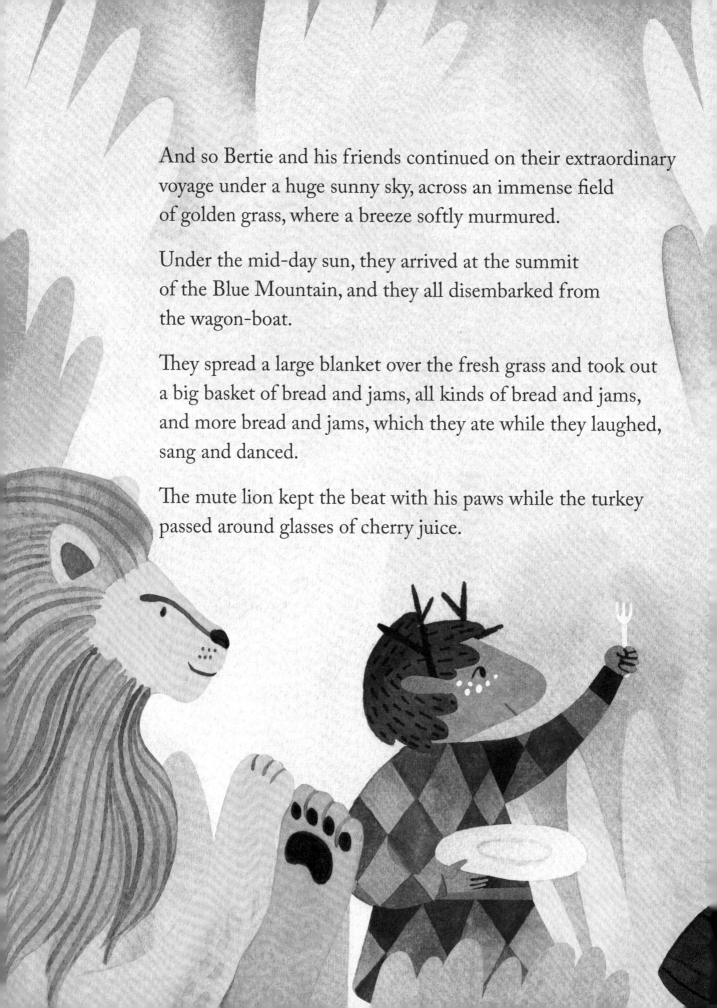

And so Bertie and his friends continued on their extraordinary voyage under a huge sunny sky, across an immense field of golden grass, where a breeze softly murmured.

Under the mid-day sun, they arrived at the summit of the Blue Mountain, and they all disembarked from the wagon-boat.

They spread a large blanket over the fresh grass and took out a big basket of bread and jams, all kinds of bread and jams, and more bread and jams, which they ate while they laughed, sang and danced.

The mute lion kept the beat with his paws while the turkey passed around glasses of cherry juice.

19 JAM

Jam from hazelnut
Belongs to the skunk
Jam with bacon
Is for the raccoon
Jam with prawn rice
Belongs to the mice
Jam that's just plain jelly
Is for the bunny

Jam with carrots
Is for the marmot
Jam from pepper
Is for the rooster
Jam and just plain
chocolate
Well, that's for me!

Marty, Minnie, Maggie, Bertie and all the animals agreed that this had been the most beautiful, fabulous, extraordinary voyage of their whole life.

From the top of the mountain, they saw that the clouds were still raining down, far away, on their little corner of the country.

Perhaps it would rain there forever and even for eternity?

And so… they were just as well to stay and settle down here, on this beautiful mountain where they now felt so marvelously, magnificently and wonderfully at home!

The Blue Mountain would be a land of new beginnings. They already loved being there!

"And," Bertie said softly to himself, "maybe we will make new, wonderful friends? Surely, there are neighbours nearby…"

20 BERTIE AND FRIENDS

We're Bertie's friends, yes we are!
The greatest friends in the world!
No bigger than a nut
Taratata
Taratata

We're Bertie's friends, yes we are!
The greatest friends in the world!
And we will never be apart
Taratata
Taratata
We're Bertie's friends, yes we are!
The greatest friends in the whole world!

Story and songs Christiane Duchesne et Jérôme Minière Illustrations Marianne Ferrer
Narration Mischa Cheeseman Singers Clerol et Geneviève Toupin Record producer and arrangements Jérôme Minière
Recorded and mixed by Jean-Sébastien Brault-Labbé at Géromini Studio Masterering Jean-Sébastien Brault-Labbé
at Studio Zodyo Artistic Director Roland Stringer Graphic design Stéphan Lorti for Haus Design
Translation of story and songs Carolyn Perkes Copy editing Ruth Joseph for Tangerine Media
Sound effects and programming Jérôme Minière
Acoustic and electric guitar, piano bass, ukulele and percussions Jérôme Minière

Thanks to Gina Brault, Catherine Mensour and Rachel Perrault

We acknowledge the financial support of FACTOR, the Government of Canada and Canada's private radio broadcasters.

A unique code for the digital download of all recordings and a printable file of the illustrated story
and lyrics is included with this book-CD. All recordings are also available on several musical streaming platforms.

ISBN-13: 978-2-925108-69-6
Ⓟ Ⓒ 2021 The Secret Mountain (Folle Avoine Productions)
Ⓚ www.lamontagnesecrete.com

All rights reserved. No part of this publication may be reproduced or transmitted in any form or by any means,
electronic or mechanical, including photocopying, recording or any information storage and retrieval system,
without permission in writing from the publisher. Printed in China.